MOTHMAN
ENCOUNTERS

TEXT + ART + DESIGN
MARK A. RANDALL

First edition: February 2023
Printed in the United States of America
ISBN: 9798378365654

www.facebook.com/markarandallcreativeartist

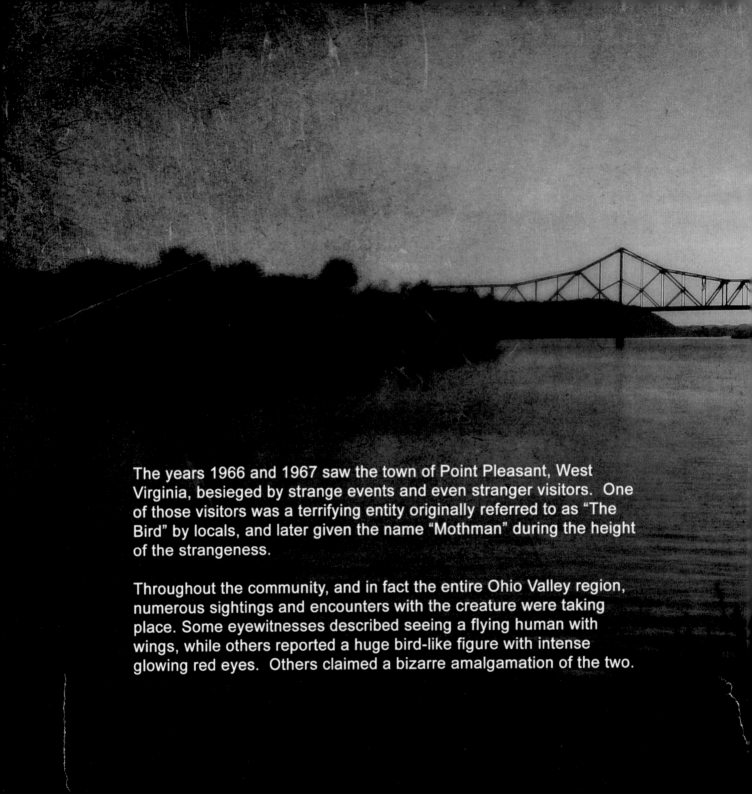

The years 1966 and 1967 saw the town of Point Pleasant, West Virginia, besieged by strange events and even stranger visitors. One of those visitors was a terrifying entity originally referred to as "The Bird" by locals, and later given the name "Mothman" during the height of the strangeness.

Throughout the community, and in fact the entire Ohio Valley region, numerous sightings and encounters with the creature were taking place. Some eyewitnesses described seeing a flying human with wings, while others reported a huge bird-like figure with intense glowing red eyes. Others claimed a bizarre amalgamation of the two.

August 1966
Point Pleasant, West Virginia

Lawrence Gray was returning home from church one evening, when
he was struck with overwhelming fear and dread. It was a sensation
that someone or something was inside his house. As he searched
from room to room, the feeling became almost unbearable. However,
he did not find anything out of place.

Around 3 am the next morning, Lawrence suddenly found himself
awake and looking out the bedroom window. As he turned his head
back across the room, he realized that something was standing in the
corner. It was a huge six-foot-tall gray figure with wings and it
seemed to give off an eerie glow. Lawrence was paralyzed with fear,
but he began thinking of Bible Scriptures, and as he did so the figure
slowly faded away.

Lawrence was certain that what he had seen was the devil himself.

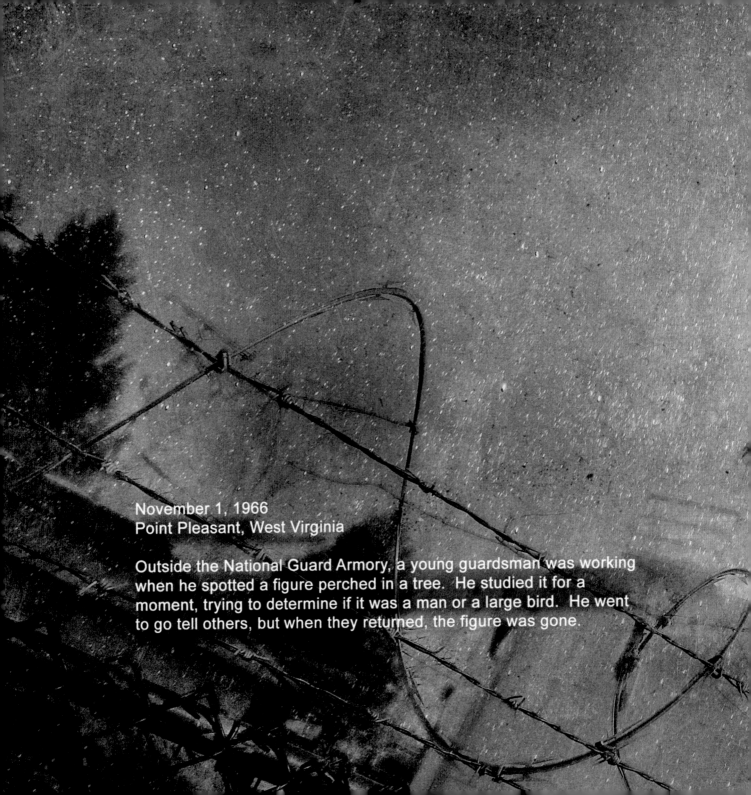

November 1, 1966
Point Pleasant, West Virginia

Outside the National Guard Armory, a young guardsman was working when he spotted a figure perched in a tree. He studied it for a moment, trying to determine if it was a man or a large bird. He went to go tell others, but when they returned, the figure was gone.

November 12, 1966
Clendenin, West Virginia

While digging a grave with four other men, Kenneth Duncan claimed
to watch as a flying man suddenly appeared and glided among the
nearby trees. The large figure was brown in color and definitely more
human-like than bird. He watched it for approximately one minute
before it flew out of sight.

November 15, 1966
Point Pleasant, West Virginia

Late one evening two young married couples- Roger and Linda
Scarberry and Steve and Mary Mallette- were cruising around the TNT
Area just north of Point Pleasant. The area, which had been a former
WWII munitions storage facility, was now a local hangout spot for
teens. As the couples neared the north power plant, they noticed a
pair of large glowing red eyes peering back at them. The figure was
at least six-feet-tall, gray in color and had large wings.

Terrified, they quickly drove away and headed back toward Point
Pleasant. It was then that they saw the creature again near a
billboard. As they passed by, the thing opened its wings, rose straight
up and began chasing them. Even though Roger's car was going
nearly 100 mph, the creature kept up with them all the way to the
edge of town before veering off into the night.

November 16, 1966
Point Pleasant, West Virginia

Marcella Bennett (along with her infant daughter Tina) and her brother
Raymond Wamsley and his wife Cathy were visiting relatives who
lived in the TNT Area. As they stepped out to leave, Raymond spotted
several strange lights in the night sky. He called out to Marcella to get
her to look, but she ignored him and walked toward the car. As she
started to unlock the car door, she suddenly noticed two legs covered
in gray feathers, and a huge dark form rose up. The thing was
human-shaped but looked more like a giant bird with feathers and
folded wings. Marcella tried to run but her legs felt paralyzed and she
fell. Finally she made it back to her feet and rushed inside the house.

Once inside, Marcella was tended to as Raymond phoned the Mason
County sheriff's department. As they waited for the police to arrive,
they heard the thing walking on the front porch and watched as it
peered in the window.

When the police finally arrived, the creature was nowhere to be found.

November 18, 1966
Point Pleasant, West Virginia

Fourteen-year-old Faye Dewitt and her siblings had just watched a
movie in Ohio when they decided to drive up the TNT Area. Faye's
sixteen-year-old brother Topper was convinced that all the commotion
over the giant bird was just someone pulling a prank.

As they pulled onto the road leading to the TNT Area, Faye realized
the creature was running (or flying) right beside their vehicle. In a
panic, Topper tried to outrun it and eventually skidded to a stop near
the north power plant. That is when the creature jumped onto the
hood of the car. It stared at them for a moment before jumping off the
car and then jumping three stories up to the top of the building.
Topper got out and began throwing chunks of coal at the creature.
When one landed near its feet, it opened its wings and jumped down
off the side. That was the last the group saw of the creature.

November 21, 1966
Charleston, West Virginia

Richard West called the police one evening to report that a winged figure was sitting on the roof of his neighbor's house. The figure appeared to be six-feet tall and dark in color with glowing red eyes. He watched it for a few minutes before it opened its wings and took off straight up like a helicopter.

November 25, 1966
Point Pleasant, West Virginia

It was the day after Thanksgiving, and Tom Ury was up early in order to make the drive from Point Pleasant back to his job in Clarksburg. He was just north of the TNT Area on Route 62 when he noticed something very strange coming over the trees. At first, he thought it was a helicopter the way it rose up, but there was no sound. He quickly realized it was a large bird with a ten to twelve-foot wingspan. It began circling his car, coming closer with each pass. He floored the gas pedal in an attempt to outrun it. Just as he reached a straight stretch of road, he saw the bird make one final pass and fly back toward the river.

November 26, 1966
St. Albans, West Virginia

Ruth Foster walked out on her front porch early one evening to find a large six-foot-tall figure in the yard. She stared in amazement at the hulking creature with blazing red eyes. Letting out a scream, she ran back inside to tell her brother-in-law. When he rushed out to investigate, the creature was gone.

November 27, 1966
New Haven, West Virginia

At about 10:30 am Sunday morning, Connie Carpenter was driving home from church when she had a terrifying encounter. She was just passing the Mason County golf course when she looked over to see a tall gray figure with flaming red eyes. Before she had time to process what was going on, large wings opened on its back and it flew straight toward her car. She was so terrified that she nearly ran her car off the road as the creature flew up and over her.

Immediately after the sighting, Connie's eyes would become red and swollen- the symptoms resembling that of exposure to welder's flash. She would also go on to have a number of unnerving episodes involving the TNT Area and the Men in Black.

November 1966
Point Pleasant, West Virginia

It was a cold November night when Bob Bosworth and Alan Coates took a motorcycle ride to the TNT Area. As they approached the north power plant, they noticed a pair of glowing red eyes staring down at them from the roof. They first thought the lights might be reflectors nailed to a board, but the eyes seemed to follow their every move.

They entered the dilapidated building and climbed the steps to the top floor. Immediately they could see the silhouette of a large figure standing in the shadows. It appeared to be six or seven- feet tall and broad-shouldered with no neck. The figure slowly approached them, crushing glass underfoot as it walked. It then turned and walked toward the rickety metal catwalks. In the darkness, the men could hear the sound of fluttering wings.

As they hurriedly sped away, they could only wonder what it was they had just encountered.

January 11, 1967
Point Pleasant, West Virginia

Early one evening, Mabel McDaniel (mother to Linda Scarberry) was
walking near Tiny's Drive-in when she spotted what looked like an
airplane flying over Route 62. As she studied it, though, she realized
it was a large brown creature with about a ten-foot wingspan and
human legs hanging down. It glided silently over Tiny's a few times
and then disappeared into the distance.

March 12, 1967
Letart Falls, Ohio

A woman and her daughter were driving home from church late one evening when they encountered what they believed to be a heavenly being. As they came around a corner, the car's headlights illuminated a large white figure. It had ten- foot wings, which were curved, and flowing white hair. It appeared for just a moment before suddenly taking flight and disappearing into the night sky. They both firmly believed this apparition to be a sign from God.

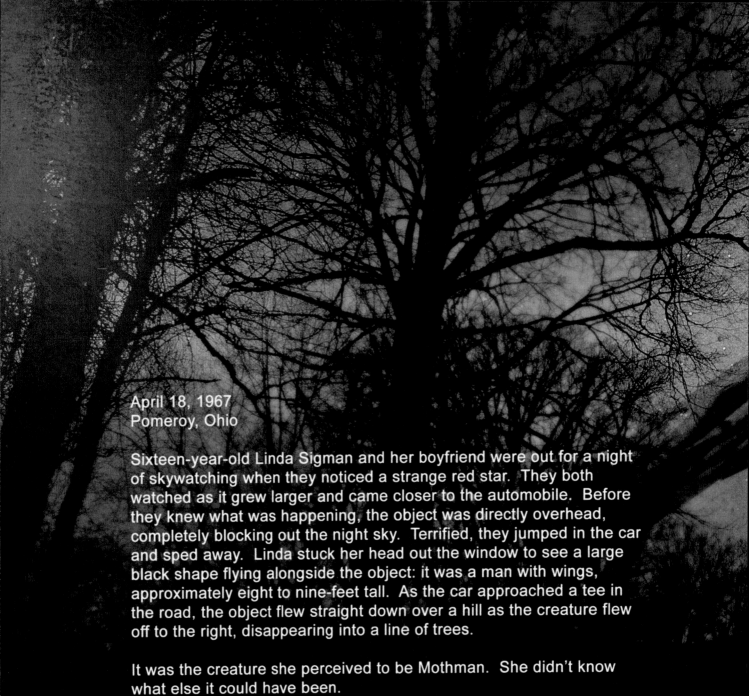

April 18, 1967
Pomeroy, Ohio

Sixteen-year-old Linda Sigman and her boyfriend were out for a night of skywatching when they noticed a strange red star. They both watched as it grew larger and came closer to the automobile. Before they knew what was happening, the object was directly overhead, completely blocking out the night sky. Terrified, they jumped in the car and sped away. Linda stuck her head out the window to see a large black shape flying alongside the object: it was a man with wings, approximately eight to nine-feet tall. As the car approached a tee in the road, the object flew straight down over a hill as the creature flew off to the right, disappearing into a line of trees.

It was the creature she perceived to be Mothman. She didn't know what else it could have been.

May 19, 1967
Point Pleasant, West Virginia

Brenda Stone and a friend were driving past the TNT Area at about
10:30 pm one evening when they saw something out of this world.
They claimed to have seen a dark shape with glowing red eyes sitting
in a tree. As the women watched, a large red object appeared in the
night sky and descended toward the tree. The creature suddenly
opened its wings, flew toward the luminous object and disappeared in
a flash. The object hovered a moment and then moved off to the
north.

June 29, June 30 and July 1, 1967
Point Pleasant, West Virginia

After her initial encounter with Mothman on November 15, 1966, Linda
Scarberry claimed to have been visited by Mothman in December
1966. She described seeing the creature sitting on the slanted roof
outside her bedroom window. It appeared with its wings folded
around itself to keep warm, and its head was turned sideways as it
looked in the window.

Mothman would appear again to Linda over three consecutive nights
in 1967. Both she and her husband Roger experienced activity on the
roof of their home. Linda again claimed to have seen the creature
sitting outside her window, its mesmerizing red eyes glowing in the
dark.

November 2, 1967
Point Pleasant, West Virginia

Virginia Thomas was in the kitchen of her home, which was located
inside the TNT Area. It was around 12:30 pm when she heard an
extremely loud squeaking sound coming from outside. She stepped
out onto the porch and saw a large shadow fall across the ground.
Suddenly her eyes caught movement of a tall dark gray figure quickly
gliding over the grass. She watched it a moment darting in and
around the igloos until it vanished into the woods.

Interestingly, Virginia's home was the same location where a year
earlier Marcella Bennett had her encounter. Virginia and Marcella
also just happened to be sisters.

November 7, 1967
Southside, West Virginia

While hunting inside the Chief Cornstalk Park, located about 13 miles
south of Point Pleasant, four hunters encountered a large gray
creature with glowing red eyes. Even though they were all armed,
they were too stunned to even raise their weapons.

After the tragedy of the Silver Bridge collapse on December 16, 1967, the sightings of Mothman became much less frequent. Although there was still the occasional sighting, there would never again be a wave that rivaled that of the one strange year when the small town was visited by a Man-Sized Bird...Creature...Something!

Made in the USA
Middletown, DE
11 March 2023

26485448R00027